Now We Have
a Baby

Text by Lois Rock
Illustrations copyright © 2004 Jane Massey
This edition copyright © 2004 Lion Hudson

The moral rights of the author and illustrator
have been asserted

A Lion Children's Book
an imprint of
Lion Hudson plc
Mayfield House, 256 Banbury Road,
Oxford OX2 7DH, England
www.lionhudson.com
ISBN-13: 978-0-7459-4885-0
ISBN-10: 0-7459-4885-5

First edition 2004
3 5 7 9 10 8 6 4 2

A catalogue record for this book is available
from the British Library

Typeset in Old Claude
Printed and bound in Singapore

Now We Have a Baby

Lois Rock

Illustrated by Jane Massey

LION
CHILDREN'S

Here is a baby,
newborn and tiny.
There are lots of
things to know
about babies.

Babies need to sleep a lot. You sometimes have to be quiet when baby is sleeping.

Babies wake up at
funny times. When
they do, they can be
very noisy.

Babies need lots of looking after. Sometimes, you will be very busy looking after baby.

Sometimes,
baby has a lot
of fun.

Everybody seems to love baby.

Sometimes,
you can feel
left out.

But every tiny baby
is a little person who
needs people to love
them.

Love helps them learn about **smiling** and **talking**.

Love helps them
learn about helping
and playing.

Love helps them learn about caring and sharing.

Love makes baby part of our family, for a family is love.

Welcome baby!

More books for young children from Lion Children's Books

You Are Very Special   *Su Box and Susie Poole*

My Very First Bible   *Lois Rock and Alex Ayliffe*

My Very First Bedtime Book   *Lois Rock and Alex Ayliffe*